For Barb Lawton
faithful witness
H.B.

For Frances
J.O.

Text copyright © 1994 by Helen E. Buckley
Illustrations copyright © 1994 by Jan Ormerod
All rights reserved. No part of this book may be reproduced or utilized in any form or by any
means, electronic or mechanical, including photocopying and recording, or by any information
storage and retrieval system, without permission in writing from the Publisher. Inquiries should
be addressed to Lothrop, Lee & Shepard Books, a division of William Morrow & Company, Inc.,
1350 Avenue of the Americas, New York, New York 10019. Printed in Hong Kong.

First Edition   1   2   3   4   5   6   7   8   9   10

Library of Congress Cataloging in Publication Data
Buckley, Helen E. Grandfather and I / by Helen Buckley : illustrated by Jan Ormerod.
p.   cm. Summary: A child considers how Grandfather is the perfect person to spend time
with because he is never in a hurry. ISBN 0-688-12533-6.—ISBN 0-688-12534-4 (lib. bdg.)
[1. Grandfathers—Fiction.]   I. Ormerod, Jan, ill.   II. Title.   PZ7.B882Gr   1994
[E]—dc20   93-22936   CIP   AC

GRANDFATHER
AND I

HELEN E. BUCKLEY • JAN ORMEROD

LOTHROP, LEE & SHEPARD BOOKS   NEW YORK

Grandfather and I
are going for a walk.
It will be a slow walk
because
Grandfather and I
never hurry.
We walk along
and walk along
and stop...
and look...
just as long as we like.

*Other people we know
are always in a hurry.
Mothers hurry.
They walk in a hurry
and talk in a hurry.
And they always want* **you** *to hurry.*

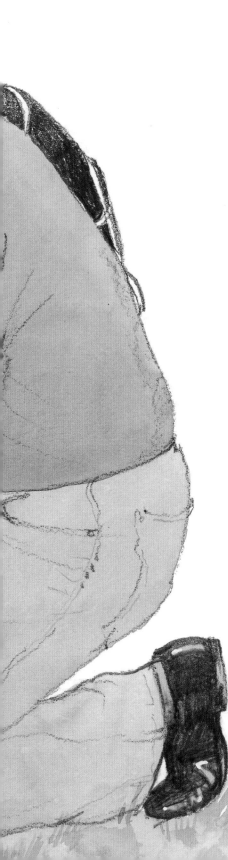

But Grandfather and I
never hurry.
We walk along
and walk along
and stop...
and look...
just as long as we like.

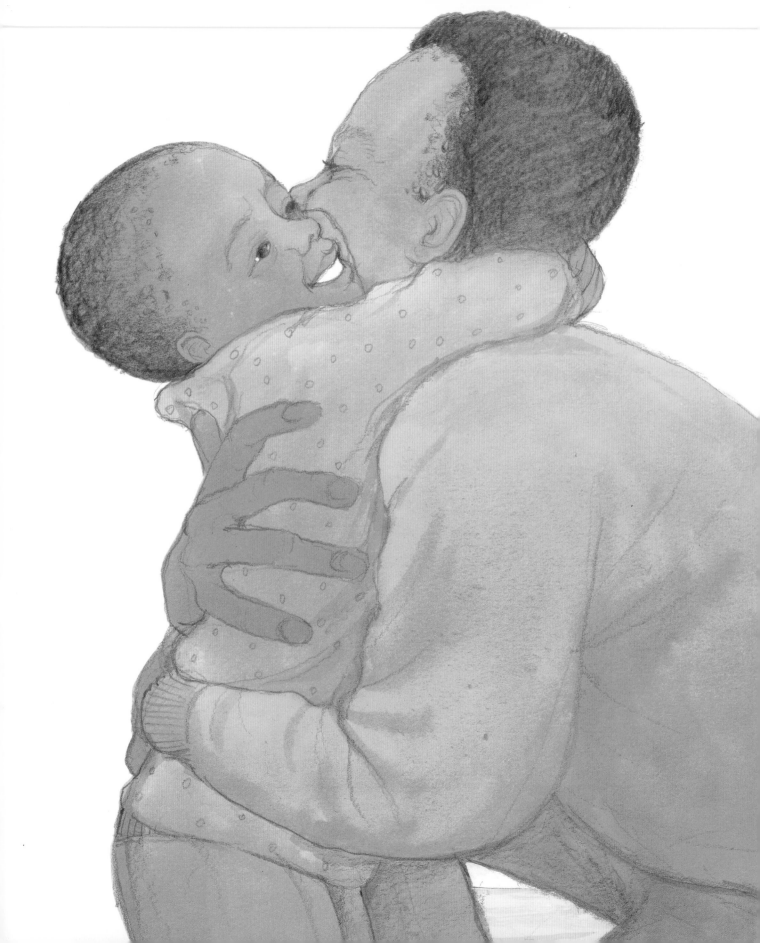

Fathers hurry.
They hurry off to work
and they hurry home again.
They hurry when they kiss you
and when they
take you for a ride.

But Grandfather and I
never hurry.
We walk along
and walk along
and stop…
and look…
just as long as we like.

Brothers and sisters hurry too.
They go so fast
they often bump into you.
And when they take you
for a walk
they are always
leaving you far behind.

But Grandfather and I
never hurry.
We walk along
and walk along
and stop...
and look...
just as long as we like.

Things hurry.
Cars and buses.
Trains and little boats.
They make noises when they hurry—
They toot whistles and blow horns.
And sometimes
scare you.

*But Grandfather and I
never hurry.
We walk along
and walk along
and stop…
and look…
just as long as we like.*

And when Grandfather and I get home,
we sit in a chair
and rock and rock...
and read a little...
and talk a little...
and look...
just as long as we like—

until somebody
tells us to hurry.